The Other Author Arthur

Sheree Fitch

illustrated by Jill Quinn

Pottersfield Press
Lawrencetown Beach
Nova Scotia, Canada

Canadian Cataloguing in Publication Data

Fitch, Sheree
      The other author Arthur
      ISBN 1-895900-20-4

I. Quinn, Jill.   II. Title.

PS8561.I86085 1999   jC813'.54   C99-950018-X
P27.F5620t 1999

Pottersfield Press gratefully acknowledges the ongoing support of the Nova Scotia Department of Education, Cultural Affairs Division, as well as the Canada Council for the Arts. We acknowledge the financial support of the Government of Canada through the Book Publishing Industry Development Program for our publishing activities.

Printed in Canada

THE CANADA COUNCIL | LE CONSEIL DES ARTS
FOR THE ARTS | DU CANADA
SINCE 1957 | DEPUIS 1957

Pottersfield Press
83 Leslie Road
East Lawrencetown
Nova Scotia, Canada, B2Z 1P8
To order, phone 1-800-NIMBUS9 (1-800-646-2879)

Reprinted 2000

Dedication

To Jane Buss, who is a writer's best friend and brings writers and schools together.

To Martha Langille, the librarian who made my African safari a reality.

To all the students, librarians and teachers who bring my books to life by reading them and who have made all my author visits exceptional.

— S.F.

To Andy, who's given me love, support and a wonderful family.

— J.Q.

Author's Note

One of my favourite authors is Budge Wilson. I've put her in this book under the name of Canary Wilson. The reference to Canary Wilson's book, *The Horse That Mooed*, is a play on the title of Budge Wilson's book, *The Cat That Barked*, also available from Pottersfield Press.

Chapter 1
Mr. Tiggle's Secret

The students and staff at Upper Milli-docket Elementary School were exceptionally excited.

They were fizzy as root beer.

They were bouncy as balloons about to burst.

They were jumpy as kangaroos.

They were expecting a visitor.

A real live author was coming to their school.

The author's name was Arthur T. Inkpen. Everyone thought this was a fine name for a writer to have.

"Arthur, the Author," said Mr. Tiggle. "It's almost like a poem, isn't it? A tongue twister? And Inkpen! Imagine! It's like he was born to be a writer!"

Mr. Tiggle loved words.

Every day he put up a new word on the bulletin board in the front hall.

He called it Mr. Tiggle's Delicious Word List.

He loved poems too.

Every day he read one over the intercom after he made the announcements. "A poem a day keeps the bugaboos away!" was his motto.

Sometimes, Mr. Tiggle even made up his own poems. His favourite poem was one about himself:

My name is Mr. Tiggle
My belly has a jiggle
I am often known to giggle
At my very own jokes!
I love the sound of children learning
And laughing as they learn
Yes, children are my very favourite folks!
BUT . . . . I expect respect
And proper conduct
Obedience to this rule:
Consideration for each other
It's what makes a school a school!

Even though Mr. Tiggle loved being a principal, he secretly dreamed of publishing a book of his own. He hoped he would be brave enough to show some of his poems to the visiting author. Miss Argyle had typed them up neatly on the school computer.

Mr. Tiggle called his collection of poems *It's a Matter of Principals!*

"That is a word joke called a pun," he explained to Miss Argyle.

Miss Argyle rolled her eyes.

"Honestly, Mr. Tiggle, I know what a pun is! I like poetry myself. Some of yours are very good, by the way."

"Some?" asked Mr. Tiggle. "Which ones?"

"I liked the first twenty the best," she said honestly.

"Then those are the ones I will show the author," smiled Mr. Tiggle.

"Do you think Arthur T. Inkpen will thike tem loo?" he asked her.

"Thike tem loo?" repeated Miss Argyle raising her eyebrows.

"I mean like them, too." Mr. Tiggle corrected himself. When he got nervous he often made a lipslip with his words.

"Relax, Mr. Tiggle. I am sure that he will love them."

This made Mr. Tiggle brave. It would be the first time he admitted his secret ambition to anyone other than Miss Argyle.

He was excited.

He was prepared.

So was everyone else at Upper Millidocket Elementary School.

Chapter 2
Be Prepared

Here's what the students and staff had been doing to get ready for the visit of the author, Arthur T. Inkpen.

Primary and Grade Ones made a huge banner to put over the door of the school.

AUTHOR DAY!
WELCOME TO UPPER MILLIDOCKET
ELEMENTARY SCHOOL

It took them a long time.

They pressed hard with their crayons to make the colours happy and bright. Then they learned a poem by heart. One of Arthur T. Inkpen's poems of course.

The Grade Sixes wrote a book of short stories and poems on the computer. They titled their book *Write On!*

The Grade Fours painted pictures of the characters in Arthur T. Inkpen's books. They decorated the walls and doors of the entire school with fantastic artwork.

The Grade Twos and Threes were doing a short play based on one of the books. Mr. Long, the music teacher, had composed a special song for the play. They were going to sing it to Mr. Inkpen.

With Miss Onyermark's help, Grade Fives had worked out a dance number. It was based on a scene from one of Arthur T. Inkpen's books. It was a jazzy number and they were proud of themselves. Miss Onyermark said they would get extra marks for gym because they had worked so hard.

For weeks, everyone knew that two short blasts of her whistle meant time for rehearsal! Her voice boomeranged throughout the school.

"Umees! Umees! And begin!"

(Umees was the nickname for all staff and students at Upper Millidocket Elementary School.)

"Work! Work! Dance Dance!
Lift those toes! Now here's your chance!
Umees are like worker bees!
Hop one two and lift those knees!
Work! Work! Work!"

Miss Onyermark worked her students hard.

But no one had worked harder than Mrs. Reed.

Mrs. Reed was the best librarian a school ever had. It was all because of her the day was about to happen.

Mrs. Reed had heard about a program called Writers In The Schools.

She contacted them and was told how to get money for the visit.

She said they wanted the author, Arthur T. Inkpen.

What a great day it was when Mrs. Reed learned that Mr. Arthur T. Inkpen had agreed to visit. Then she began preparing.

This is what she did.

She ordered all the author's books.

She asked every class and teacher to read almost every book.

Arthur T. Inkpen had six published books.

Everybody's favourite was *If Mr. Fix-it Can't Fix-it, Who Can?*

"We will read and draw and sing and paint before he comes. We will ask him questions when he gets here. We will have a special lunch! It will be a celebration of books and reading and imagination!" Mrs. Reed said to everyone at assembly.

"And words!" shouted Mr. Tiggle.

"Of course! Words! Words! Wonderful words and the worlds that words can bring us!" agreed Mrs. Reed.

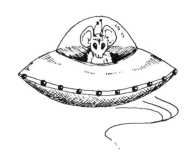

Chapter 3
A Little Bit Nervous

Mrs. Reed was the only one at the school who had ever met a real live author before.

She often met authors at library conferences.

She bought books for the school library using her own money.

She stood in long line-ups to get the real authors sign them.

She had a special shelf in the library for books signed by live authors. There were a few books signed by dead authors, too.

But even Mrs. Reed was a little bit nervous about the visit. She never ever thought an author would come to Upper Millidocket Elementary School. It was a two-hour drive from the city. She talked to the author on the phone before he visited.

"It's quite a long drive," she said. "I will fax you a map."

"That would be great," said the author. "Actually, I don't mind the drive at all. Gives me time to think. A map is a good idea, however. I have been known to get lost at times."

"Mr. Arthur T. Inkpen said he liked driving because it gave him time to think," she told the Grade Sixes in library period. "Writers do a lot of thinking."

"Doesn't he have a chauffeur?" asked Aaron McDougall. "If he is a famous writer he must be rich!"

"Not necessarily," said Mrs. Reed. "In fact, I have heard a lot of writers are actually quite poor."

"Then why do they do it?" asked Aaron.

"There are other rewards besides money," said Mrs. Reed.

"Like what?"

"Well, I would imagine just knowing some-one reads your books is quite a thrill in itself."

Yeah, right, thought Aaron. He wanted to make lots of money when he grew up. In fact, he planned on being a millionaire.

"What are authors like anyhow?" asked Angela when she was returning a library book. It was the day before Arthur T. Inkpen was due to arrive.

Mrs. Reed smiled and thought for a moment.

"They are just like people. In fact they are people. Some are men. Some are women. Some of them are young and some of them are old and some of them are in between. Some of them are tall, some are short. Some are shy. Some are very sure of themselves. Some of them are funny and some of them are serious. Some of them are all those things at once."

How could you be tall and short at the same time, wondered Angela.

Or a man and a woman?

Angela laughed until she snorted through her nose. She pictured some sort of alien in her head.

Mrs. Reed continued. "Snowflakes!" she shouted. "Authors are like snowflakes! No two are exactly alike."

Angela knew she was supposed to believe that no two snowflakes were alike. Mr. Potion had said so in science class. But Angela did not believe this.

"Has anyone ever seen all the snowflakes that have ever fallen?" she had asked Mr. Potion. Mr. Potion scratched his head.

"And what if some of the snowflakes that have fallen and melted are like some of the ones that come after. How do we know that no two snowflakes are alike for sure?"

"Angela, Angela, Angela," sighed Mr. Potion. "You ask such good questions." But he did not answer her.

Secretly, Angela was a bit disappointed that it was Arthur T. Inkpen who was coming to the school.

She had a favourite author and it wasn't him.

Angela's favourite author was Canary Wilson.

But maybe Mr. Inkpen knows Canary Wilson, she thought to herself. In fact, that is going to be the question I will ask him. Even meeting someone who knew her favourite author would be neat, she decided.

"Do a lot of authors know other authors?" she asked Mrs. Reed.

"I imagine they must," said Mrs. Reed. "Now really, I must finish getting ready, okay, Angela?"

"Okay," said Angela. Then she smiled at Mrs. Reed. "The library looks the best ever!"

"You think Arthur T. Inkpen will like it, too?" Mrs. Reed asked Angela.

"He will absolutely love it," said Angela.

Mrs. Reed let out a happy whistle through her teeth. That Angela is such a sweet child, she thought to herself, to notice what I have done.

It was hard not to.

Chapter 4
Really Ready

Mrs. Reed had polished and dusted.

She had arranged and rearranged her most beautiful books for display.

She had Canadian flags sticking out of the covers of all of the author's books. (That's because the author was Canadian.)

She even got fresh flowers for the library in honour of Arthur T. Inkpen's visit. Mr. Bob, the custodian, pushed back library shelves so the students would be able to gather on the floor together. He arranged chairs for the teachers at the back of the room.

Mrs. Reed's husband, Arnie, had come in the night before to help her put the finishing touches to the decorations. He blew up six balloons and tied them to the special author's chair.

All of Arthur T. Inkpen's books were set up on a table at the front of the room beside the chair.

Finally, the day they had been planning and waiting for had almost arrived.

Mr. Tiggle walked around his school the night before the visit, admiring the artwork and preparations. "The author will be impressed, I know he will. Upper Millidocket Elementary School is an exceptional school."

He had his collection of poems tucked tightly underneath his arm. As he drove to his home he recited his favourite poem to himself. *"My name is Mr. Tiggle, my belly has a jiggle. . ."*

He kept reciting his poem until it was time for bed. Then, as if he was tucking a baby into bed, he gently placed the poems under his pillow. Just before he fell asleep, he bolted wide awake.

"I was so busy today! I forgot to say my poem over the intercom this morning! But wait a minute . . . it was another wonderful Upper Millidocket Elementary School day today. Not a

bugaboo in sight." He lay back in his bed. He couldn't help wondering if the bugaboos would wait to invade the school tomorrow.

"Nonsense," he muttered to himself. He tried to think a happy thought. He fell asleep dreaming of what the front cover of his book might look like some day.

In her bed, Mrs. Reed tossed and turned wondering if she had forgotten anything. She wanted everything to be perfect.

A real live author was coming all the way out to their little school by the sea. Arthur T. Inkpen would be the most famous and the most exciting visitor they had ever had at Upper Millidocket Elementary School.

Little did they know that this was going to be an author visit like no school had ever had before.

Or any other author, either.

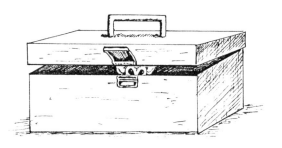

Chapter 5
The Earlier the Better?

Here's what happened.

The night before Author Day the furnace stopped working. Mr. Bob, the school custodian, noticed it first thing in the morning.

"I feel like I'm in an igloo in my birthday suit," he muttered to himself. He could see his breath when he talked. Mr. Bob often talked out loud to himself.

He put wood in the woodstove, thinking how lucky they were to have a back-up heating system.

"That'll do for a bit, I think."

He called the oil company.

"Can you send someone to fix the furnace here at Upper Millidocket Elementary School?"

"No problem. Right away," chirped the woman on the phone. "We'll get your furnace working so you won't have to cancel school." Mr. Bob thought how disappointed the students and teachers would be. Everyone liked to get the day off school now and then.

He forgot about the author visit. This was one day everyone would have been very disappointed if school was called off.

After all those plans.

After all that waiting.

Mr. Bob made himself a cup of coffee and sat down.

He enjoyed the crackle of the woodstove and the smell of wood burning. "Just like the good old days," he sighed.

After he finished his coffee, he began sweeping the floors.

At exactly 7:30, there was a loud knock on the front door.

"That furnace man got here faster than a rabbit chased by a pack of hungry wolves," said Mr. Bob. "Now that's what I call service."

At the door stood a man with a toolbox in one hand and a briefcase in the other.

"Am I glad to see you," said Mr. Bob.

"Thank you. It's nice to meet you too," said the man. "I know I'm rather early but I always say the earlier the better!"

"I couldn't agree with you more . . . the earlier the better," said Mr. Bob. "After all, we have to get things started so we can get warmed up."

The man, who was really Arthur T. Inkpen, smiled proudly. He thought Mr. Bob was giving him a compliment. He liked to know his books warmed the hearts of his readers.

"Well, I'll take you to the furnace room right away," said Mr. Bob. "I've got the wood-stove going, so it's warm in there. Maybe you'd like a cup of coffee before you begin?"

"That would be great," said Arthur T. Inkpen. He wondered why he wasn't taken to the staff room like in most schools.

He took off his coat. He was wearing over-alls. They were just like regular worker overalls but they were bright green and orange. Over the left pocket was a name. It said, "Mr. Fix-it."

Arthur T. Inkpen had come dressed as Mr. Fix-it, his most famous character. It is easy to understand why Mr. Bob made the mistake that he did. The man before him had a toolbox. He was wearing overalls. Strangely coloured overalls, but still, they were overalls.

"Quite the get-up you've got on there," said Mr. Bob. "Fellow almost needs a pair of sunglasses to look at you."

"My wife made them for me," said Arthur T. Inkpen. "She thought the students would like them."

Mr. Bob did not really know why the students would care what the furnace man was wearing. But he was polite. All he said was, "Your wife is very good at sewing."

"Actually," said Arthur T. Inkpen, "she has made me many costumes."

"For Hallowe'en?" asked Mr. Bob.

"No, I usually dress up for my work."

Mr. Bob thought this was the strangest furnace repair man he had ever met.

"Well, look. I've got to run to the high school up the road. Hope you don't mind me leaving you here."

"Not at all," said Mr. Inkpen. "It's very quiet here. I might even get some work done before school starts."

"Well, that would be ideal," said Mr. Bob. "But finish your coffee at least. Bye."

Mr. Bob left Arthur T. Inkpen in the furnace room of the school. Two doors closed behind him as he left.

Arthur T. Inkpen loved the smell of burning wood. He loved the sound of a crackling fire. "Now this," he sighed, "is a writer's dream. No distractions whatsoever."

Chapter 6
Lost in Africa

Arthur T. Inkpen opened his toolbox. Here's what he took out.

One pad of paper. With lines.

One pencil. His little stub of a pencil that fit perfectly between his fingers.

His best friend. That's right, Arthur T. Inkpen's best friend was inside that toolbox, too. Arthur T. Inkpen always told students his best friend was his eraser.

"That's because my ideas and feelings never come all the way out from my head and my heart, down my arm, out my hand, and out the end of my pencil perfectly the first time. I

have to write and cross out, write and erase, write and write many times. Sometimes just to get one line exactly the way that I want it. So yes — you could say my best friend is my eraser. I have gone through many erasers in my lifetime as a writer."

The students were amazed when Arthur T. Inkpen told them how long it took for him to write just one book. "But some writers work faster than me," he said. "We all have our own way of doing things."

Lately, however, just getting a chance to write had been a problem for Arthur T. Inkpen.

At home his phone had been ringing, the mail was piled high, and his baby had been teething.

"I'll bet I can get a whole hour's worth of writing done before school starts," he smiled to himself, taking another deep gulp of coffee. "I can start that new book I've been thinking about. Ah, yes, the earlier the better."

"I want to tell you a story about a friend of mine," he began. *"Her name is Gertrude. Gert, for short. Gertie to her friends. Gertie is a gecko who lives in and around a house in Nairobi, Kenya, underneath a baobab tree."*

Soon Arthur T. Inkpen was lost. Lost completely in his own imagination and the memories of his recent trip to Africa.

He did not hear the stomp of feet above his head.

Or if he did, perhaps he just thought it was the elephants he was writing about in his story.

He did not hear the first school bell ring.

Or if he did, it was like a mouse squeak compared to the zinging of his brain and the singing of his heart. Great ideas for his story came tumbling and spilling out the end of his pencil onto that page.

That's how the mix-up began.

Arthur T. Inkpen, the long-awaited visitor, sat happily writing in the furnace room of Upper Millidocket Elementary School.

Chapter 7
Another Case of Mistaken Identity

At 8:45, Arthur Good the furnace man roared into the schoolyard at Upper Millidocket Elementary School.

Until then, both Mr. Tiggle and Mrs. Reed had feared the author had gotten lost.

"But my map was a good one," Mrs. Reed said to herself, glancing at the clock in the library and arranging the flowers once more.

Then Mr. Tiggle saw a man walking up to the front door of the school.

"He looks just like Mr. Fix-it!" he said.

Miss Argyle looked out the window.

"He's even got grease on his face," she said. "Isn't that a little bit much?

"Not at all," said Mr. Tiggle. "Some authors really get into their characters. The students will be thrilled."

He clutched his poems to his heart and hurried from his office.

Simon Archer was at the door before Mr. Tiggle. He was the official greeter.

"Are you the other?" asked Simon. Simon often got words mixed up when he was nervous. Besides, the words other and author and arthur were not easy to tell apart, either. "I mean, are you the arthur?"

"Yes, I am," said the furnace man, suprised. His name was Arthur Good.

"But how did you know my name?"

"Oh, we've heard all about you!"

It was Mr. Tiggle. He shook Arthur Good's hand up and down like a water pump.

"You have?" Arthur Good scratched his forehead.

"For years!" beamed Mr. Tiggle. He patted Simon on the head. "Thank you Simon, for welcoming our guest."

"Yes, thank you, young man. I am not used to being given such a welcome when I do my work."

"Well your work is well known to all of us out here at Upper Millidocket Elementary School."

Mr. Good was pleased. He had been working very hard lately and it wasn't often people knew how hard a furnace repair man worked.

"So good . . . you're here!" exclaimed Mr. Tiggle, still nervous.

"Yes, I am." They even know my last name thought Arthur Good. I guess I do have a reputation to live up to at this place.

"Just let me say again, welcome to Upper Millidocket Elementary School. It seems like we've been waiting for you forever!" Mr. Tiggle beamed.

"Tried to get here soon as I could," harrumphed Arthur Good. People were always complaining about not getting service when they wanted it. But a man can only be fixing one furnace at a time, he often said to himself. Don't people understand? I just take the calls in the order they come!

Mr. Tiggle, who was a very sensitive man, knew that he said something wrong.

"Oh, no . . . you're in tots of lime," stumbled Mr. Tiggle.

"Tots of lime?"

"I mean lits of time," gulped Tiggle. Oh dear, he was getting all tongue-tangled now. "LOTS OF TIME!" he shouted out.

Arthur Good was getting impatient. What an odd man, he thought to himself. Then again, principals are people too. Besides, as his dear mother loved to say, "It takes all kinds to make the world spin around." At the moment, however, Mr. Tiggle was making his *head* spin around.

Chapter 8
Why the Truth Did Not Get Discovered

"Just show me where to go, sir." Arthur Good would just do his job and get out of this place as soon as possible. At least he would try.

"Please, you can call me . . . Mr. Tiggle," said Mr. Tiggle. "How about we go to the staff room first? You can have cup of coffee and relax before you start."

Arthur Good blinked twice. Most folks never offered him coffee. Time was money. Most people wanted him in and out of a place as fast as possible.

"I'd prefer tea, if you have it," said Arthur Good. "I've been up since early and it's mighty cold out there."

"Tea, tea. We have tea, too. Two for tea, get it? I am a bit of a wordsmith myself." Arthur Good made no reply.

Mr. Tiggle led the way to the staff room. He did not have the nerve to ask the author to look at his poems yet.

"The staff would like to meet you as well," was all he said instead.

"They would?"

"Oh, yes. After all, we are working you hard today."

"It's no big deal," said Arthur Good.

"Oh, it's a very big deal to us," laughed Mr. Tiggle. "And don't get me wrong, either. We want you to have fun, too!"

"Well, it's usually pretty dirty work," replied Mr. Good. "But actually, I do enjoy it very much. It's always a challenge."

Mr. Tiggle giggled.

"Dirty work. Dirty work, I get it, Mr. Fix-it!" he winked. "What a great sense of humour you have!"

He slapped Arthur Good on the back like he was a football player and continued laughing.

He laughed so hard he had to stop and wipe his brow. Arthur Good just wanted to go home.

The teachers all stopped talking when the two men entered the staff room.

Mr. Tiggle was grinning like he was about to say *Chee-ee-ese* for a photo. He had grease smeared all over his face by this time.

Mr. Good looked like a man trying to solve a crossword puzzle.

The teachers were surprised by the appearance of the author but they had been warned by Mrs. Reed that writers were sometimes a bit unusual in their ways. "Eccentric," was the word she had used.

"Still," muttered Mrs. Graves to Mr. Long, "he smells like gasoline. What sort of role model is this for our students?"

Chapter 9
More Tongue Tangling Trouble

Mr. Tiggle went around the room and introduced every one by name. But he didn't say this is Mr. Arthur T. Inkpen. If he had, the whole day might have gone quite differently.

"And, of course, you all know who this is," is what he said. Everyone grinned and nodded.

"We sure do!" they said. "We're so excited you're here at last."

Arthur Good wrinkled his brow and got out his notebook of work orders and a pencil.

"How long have you been waiting?"

"Weeks and weeks," said Mrs. Day, the resource teacher.

Arthur Good was alarmed. He wrote something in his notebook.

All the teachers were impressed. Always working. A writer was always working, they told their students. Now they had proof.

"You must have been pretty cold," said Arthur Good.

"Yes, the weather's been unusually cold for this time of year," said Mr. Potion, the science teacher.

"El Nino has been changing our weather patterns. We have had to use our woodstove often this winter."

"Oh, I see." Mr. Good was relieved. That was it. They had a woodstove to keep them warm when the furnace was not working. He scribbled down the notes and put his notebook away.

"Coffee, sir? A carrot muffin before you begin?"

What a friendly bunch, thought Arthur Good.

"Tea, please. Do you always eat so well in this school?"

"Actually, I baked them specially for your visit," said Miss Argyle.

"Well, well, well, I don't know what to say," said Arthur Good. I guess they just don't get many people out this way, is what he was thinking to himself.

Mrs. Reed sat down next to Arthur Good at the table.

She was wearing her new magenta dress and her new perfume, Oh La La. Just a little dab, because there were many people who were allergic to perfume. But she was glad, because the author smelled like a gas station.

Mrs. Reed had on new shoes covered with fur that looked like Dalmatian dogs or cows, perhaps. There was a cow in one of Arthur T. Inkpen's poems.

Mrs. Reed's husband, Arnie, had teased her that morning before she left her house.

"Now, Mrs. Reed," he said, "I just hope you don't have any plans about running away with that author."

"I just wanted to look my best," she said, kissing his nose.

"You are the best," said her husband. "And you look beautiful."

"No, you are the best," she said. "Why don't you drop in at lunch for our pot luck? The parents have been cooking all week long." Mr. Reed said he'd try to get away from his work to do just that.

Now the author was right in front of her. Mrs. Reed cleared her throat. The author was a handsome enough man, but sort of oily, she decided.

She wanted to shake Arthur T. Inkpen's hand but she didn't want to get grease on her new dress. But she was brave.

"I am Mrs. Reed, the librarian. I am the one who called you."

Arthur Good the furnace man wiped his hands on his overalls and shook her hand. Mrs. Reed sure doesn't look like the librarian we had when I went to school, he was thinking to himself.

"Pleased to meet you. I am glad you called."

"We heard you were wonderful," she said. Then she got very business-like.

"So . . . everyone will come into the library at nine," she said. "They all want to meet you, as you can tell."

She pointed to the window of the staff room. Almost every student in the school had their noses pressed up against the window and were trying to look in. They were waving. "Hi, author. Hi, author!" they shouted.

Arthur Good thought they were saying Arthur, not author. So he waved back.

"Hi, there," said Mr. Good. So much attention. It felt weird and wonderful at the same time.

"But do we have time to go to the library?" he asked Mr. Tiggle.

"Of course," replied Mr. Tiggle. "We have all lay dong-day long!"

Just then the second school bell rang. The teachers disappeared off to their classes. Mr. Tiggle was called to the telephone.

Mrs. Reed poured Arthur Good another cup of tea.

"Five minutes and then you start, all right? I'll come get you. I'm sure you want some quiet time alone before you begin," said Mrs. Reed.

She left the room.

A cloud of Oh La La lingered behind her.

Quiet time? thought Arthur Good. Besides, it wasn't very quiet at that time of day in any school.

He watched as the children lined up to come into the school. They reminded him of a bowlful of dancing jellybeans. Then their laughter filled the halls outside the staff room.

It really was an exceptional school.

If they had all day, well, so did he. Unless he got a call to go some place else.

May as well do what they want, he thought.

He put his dirty teacup on the counter along with the others.

Besides, I can't fix the furnace until they take me to it, he giggled and shrugged.

Then he reached for another muffin.

Chapter 10
The Safari in the Furnace Room

"I'm hungry," muttered Arthur T. Inkpen. That is because he heard his stomach growl very loudly. He opened his briefcase and took out the bananas he always brought for recess when he visited schools.

"I wonder what time it is."

Arthur T. Inkpen never wore a watch.

He had tried all his life to wear one and even when he did, he forgot to look at it.

"Just one of my idiosyncrasies," he admitted once to his wife.

"Idio-what?" she replied. "You and your words!"

"Habits," her husband smiled. "Odd habits, in fact."

"Well, I have my own, I guess," Mrs. Inkpen giggled. At the time she was standing on her head doing yoga exercises.

The taste of bananas reminded Arthur T. Inkpen of monkeys. Tastes and smells could do that to him. So then he was back to his story.

At that moment, he was in the sweltering heat of Africa.

He was on safari with his character, Gertie the gecko.

The driver of the safari jeep was Rupert, a baboon.

The author did not notice the room was getting colder.

In fact, he wrote:

The sun shone over the savannah. Gertrude put on her sunglasses to protect her eyes from the glare. She wiped her brow with a handkerchief and took a sip of water.

"Are you all right?" asked Rupert the baboon. "We don't get many old geckos on safari, you know."

"I am not that old," said Gertie. "I'm just hot. And excited. I'm sure I heard lions growl."

"So you did," whispered Rupert, "Look!"

Arthur T. Inkpen gripped his pencil. He often got so excited when he was writing that he had to stop and go back to the beginning of his story before he could continue. He was remembering what it was like when he saw lions for the first time.

So he got lost again.

Lost in the middle of his African safari, just as the bell rang to call the students into the library.

Chapter 11
Arthur Reading

"Please sit down on your bottoms and show me what quiet students you can be," said Mrs. Reed as the students and staff entered the library.

The students did as they were told. The Grade Sixes wondered why they couldn't sit on chairs like the adults.

"Get away from me, Aaron," said Prissy Douglas.

"No problem," said Aaron and moved on the other side of her.

Secretly, Aaron had a crush on Prissy. Every time he tried to be nice to her, he ended up doing something that made her nose scrunch up with disgust.

It's as if I smell like potato peelings or something, he thought to himself. Well, today he would show her. He had some very good questions to ask the author. Prissy Douglas would be impressed. He was sure of it.

"Now I will go get Arthur T. Inkpen, boys and girls, and we will begin."

Mrs. Reed's high heel shoes covered with spotted fur made a click-clack sound, as if she were dancing through the halls.

Arthur Good was eating a third muffin when Mrs. Reed appeared at the staff room door.

"Well, they are all waiting anxiously," she smiled at the furnace man.

Arthur Good followed along behind Mrs. Reed, sniffing in the aroma of her wonderful perfume.

Mrs. Reed wished she had a clothespin for her nose.

Just before they went into the library, Mr. Tiggle grabbed Arthur Good's arm.

"These are my poems," he whispered. "I hope you don't mind, but I want to give them to you. Maybe you could tell me what you think of

them. Not today of course, but whenever you have time."

"Poems? You write poems?"

"I know. Everyone thinks a principal is just someone who makes rules. But I have a deep love of the written word. As I know you do. I would very much value your opinion. I know you have a lot of experience going into schools and that is what my poems are all about."

"Well, I'm certainly no expert when it comes to poetry," said Mr. Good.

"Of course you are. So modest, too!" replied Mr. Tiggle. He flipped through some pages.

"Here's my favourite. I'll do it for you," said Mr. Tiggle.

My tame is Mr. Niggle, my jelly has a biggle
I am often known to jiggle at my very own gokes

Mr. Good began to giggle. This was the strangest morning of his life.

"Mr. Tiggle, puh-leese!" said Mrs. Reed.

Mr. Tiggle stopped reciting and said, "Of course, let's begin. Maybe we will finish this discussion at lunch, then?" he asked hopefully.

Arthur Good just stared straight ahead. Lunch?

"I don't know if that's possible," said Arthur Good truthfully. "I'll think about it though."

Mr. Tiggle was crushed.

"Like I said, you could take them home with you and then get back to me later, if that is more convenient."

When they entered the library a hush fell over the students. Some of them waved. Some of them whispered excitedly to the friend beside them.

He's dressed as Mr. Fix-it, thought Angela.

"What's that smell?" said Prissy. She looked right at Aaron.

"What smell?" Then he sniffed. "Yeah," he said, "what is that smell?"

"Shh!" hissed Mrs. Reed, fearful the author would hear. But it was true. The library smelled like a gas station, and it was obvious that the author was the fuel pump.

Mr. Tiggle went to the front of the room and began.

"Goys and Birls. Today is the way we have been daiting for."

There he goes, thought Miss Argyle.

"He's talking Tiggle-ese again," whispered the students. "He must be very nervous."

"We all know who this is. Thank you for scoming to our cool. Before you begin, we have a surprise for you."

The Primary teacher, Mrs. Livetti, jumped up.

"In honour of your visit, the Primaries and Grade Ones have done something special. One, two, three," she said and clapped her hands.

All together the Primaries and Grade Ones stood up. They put on bouncy bumblebee headbands.

"In honor of the *The Bumblebee Who Bumbled*," said Mrs. Livetti, "a choral recitation."

The Bumblebee Who Bumbled was one of Arthur T. Inkpen's most famous poems. The Grade Ones and Primaries began when Mrs. Livetti said "Begin!"

After the students were finished their performance, Mrs. Reed told the furnace man, "So there we have it, your official welcome! Now, it's your turn."

Arthur Good looked into the sea of faces in front of him. "My turn?" he said.

Everyone nodded and began to clap.

"But what do you want me to do?"

"Why, read of course!" said Mrs. Reed.

Arthur Good froze stiff as an icicle.

Maybe he has stage fright, thought Mrs. Reed.

"Read?" repeated Arthur Good.

"Well, of course, you can do whatever you want to."

"I would like to fix the furnace," said the furnace man.

Everyone started to laugh.

Mrs. Reed clapped her hands together. "Oh, yes!" she said. "We were hoping you would read *If Mr. Fix-it Can't Fix it, Who Can?* It's right behind you."

She handed the Arthur Good the book.

It just so happened that Mr. Good had been given the book by his two nephews the Christmas before last. Inside the cover of the book they had written:

To Uncle Arthur
the best Mr. Fix-it that ever was,
Love, Tosh and Tag

Arthur Good liked this book very much.

He almost knew it by heart.

So he cracked open the book. He began to read.

It was not an author reading. Not exactly.

It was an Arthur reading. Not Arthur T. Inkpen, either. Arthur Good. The other Arthur who was not an author. That was not good.

In fact, here's how it was at that moment at Upper Millidocket Elementary School. It was enough to take your breath away.

Arthur Good, the furnace man was reading a book about a man who fixed things and everyone thought he was the author, but the author, Arthur T. Inkpen, was in the furnace room not fixing the furnace but he was fixing the wheel on the jeep that had broken down on safari which was happening in the story he was writing, which he now felt would be his next bestseller, so this meant he was completely lost in his world of words and no one except Mr. Bob who was sweeping the floors and whistling at the high school knew that he was there and all Mr. Bob knew was that he had left a man to fix the furnace at Upper Millidocket Elementary School and that sometimes furnace men wore overalls that were neon orange and green. That's all.

Chapter 12
The Heart of Darkness

For the next twenty minutes, two stories were being told at the same time at Upper Millidocket Elementary School.

One was being read.

One was being written.

One was being heard my many.

One was being heard by whatever creatures might have been hiding inside the furnace room of Upper Millidocket Elementary School.

Arthur T. Inkpen decided that the wheel on the safari jeep could not be fixed. There was no Mr. Fix-it in his story at the moment. So, he was trying to find a way to describe being in the darkness of Africa where wild animals roamed.

He wrote:

The dark was dark as the mouth of a killer whale.

Then he crossed that out.

He wrote a new line:

The dark was dark as a night without a moon. No stars. No streetlights. There were only quick flickers of lights in the distance. Gertie knew they were the gleaming eyes of wild animals. Animals that thought geckos were delicious.

Arthur T. Inkpen read that over. He sighed deeply. He erased the whole thing. This time he wrote:

The dark was the dark of an African night without a moon or even stars. It was the heart of darkness itself. The screech of baboons, the growl of cheetahs, the thundering sounds of elephants snoring, and the screams of hungry hyenas could be heard in the distance. Gertie the gecko shivered. I wanted adventure, she thought to herself, but not this much adventure!

Arthur T. Inkpen's hands were sweating. His heart was a bongo drum beating out an urgent SOS. He gripped his pencil as if it was a sword that could protect him from wild animals. Sometimes he scared himself when he wrote. This was one of those times. "Be brave," he whispered to himself. "Have courage." Not knowing what would happen next, the fearless author wrote on.

And on. And on.

Chapter 13
The Broken Heart

Arthur Good read on and on and on.

He was having a grand old time.

He loved the story of Mr. Fix-it. It began when Mr. Fix-it was a little boy, always getting into trouble because he broke everything. One day, he broke his arm. After watching the doctor fix him all up, the little boy decided he would never break anything again.

Arthur Good read this part with great feeling and emotion.

"I will not break things, I will make things. I will not take things apart, I will put things together!" And he did. He grew up to be known

as Mr. Fix-it, the man who could fix anything.
Whenever anything was broken people said,
"Let's go see Mr. Fix-it."

After all:

If Mr. Fix-it can't fix-it, who can?

The students and teachers all chimed in
together at this part of the story.

Arthur Good got really warmed up as the
story continued. He even started to do the
voices of different characters. He was coming up
to a very important part of this story.

Then one day, a woman knocked on Mr.
Fix-it's door. Her eyes drooped like a beagle
dog's and her voice scraped like sandpaper.

"My name is Mary, but I am sad. I have
heard you can fix anything that is broken."

Mr. Good made his voice all scratchy and
like a woman's. Everybody laughed.

"Well, I do my best," said Mr. Fix-it, trying
to be modest. "You know what they say about
me?"

If Mr. Fix-it can't fix-it who can?

Again, everyone yelled this together.

What a difference it was, to read out loud
to someone.

Arthur Good liked this a lot. Most days
when he worked, it was only the furnace that

hummed to him. He made his voice weepy for the next part.

"Well," said Mary, who was not merry but sad, "my heart is broken. It has been for a very long time. Can you fix a broken heart, Mr. Fix-it? I have money. Lots of money. I am a millionaire. I will pay you well."

"Yes!" shouted out Aaron McDougall, "A millionaire, like I'm gonna be!"

Everybody laughed.

"Really?" smiled Arthur Good at Aaron.

"I hope so," said Aaron.

"I just bet you will, you look very determined. Go for what you dream about!"

Aaron looked over at Prissy and Prissy looked over at Aaron and everybody went "Prissy and Aaron up in a tree, k-i-s-s–"

"Umees! Let our visitor finish the story!" It was Mrs. Reed.

Arthur Good found his place in the book and began again.

"I have never been asked to fix a broken heart before. I'm not sure I know how. I will have to think. Hard. Please come back tomorrow."

I will find a way, said Mr. Fix-it to himself. After all,

if Mr. Fix-it can't fix-it, who can?

Arthur Good loved all of this enthusiasm. He knew what was coming next in the story. It turns out that this time Mr. Fix-it is at a loss. A boy named Matthew who wants to be just like Mr. Fix-it when he grows up, tells Mr. Fix-it he thinks he knows what will fix the broken heart: *"Hugs, kisses, whispers, whiskers and lots of chocolate candy. Love! Mr. Fix-it. Love!"*

"Yuck!" said all the Grade Six boys at this point in the story. Aaron said it the loudest.

"Ahh," said all the girls. Prissy scrunched up her nose at Aaron McDougall.

After a long search, where Mr. Fix-it goes looking for love to fix sad Mary's broken heart, he discovers love has been hiding in his own lonely heart all along. He gives Mary a kitten, then they share a box of chocolates. They get married and have a baby who breaks everything.

The story ended.

"So Mr. Fix-it was kept extremely busy. After all,

if Mr. Fix-it can't fix it, who can?"

There was much clapping.

Arthur Good bowed.

Then the Grade Fives did their jazz number. Mrs. Onyermark was so proud, she almost cried. Arthur Good gave them a standing ovation.

Mr. Tiggle felt an itch of some unfamilar feeling.

The Grade Sixes presented their book of writing.

Arthur Good looked through it thoughtfully.

Mr. Tiggle began to scratch his head.

The Grade Threes did their play. Mr. Long conducted the song and took compliments for being such a great composer.

Mr. Tiggle was taking deep breaths. He was . . . was he . . . could he be . . . jealous? If anyone had been paying any attention to him, they would have noticed his face had turned the colour of canned peas.

"And now," said Mrs. Reed, "it's question time."

"Who has a question?" Almost everyone's hand went up at once.

They were prepared.

Arthur Good was scared.

A surprise quiz! He'd never been very good at those.

But smiling, the fearless furnace man turned to the first student.

Chapter 14
All Because of a T and a D and a Snowplow

"How long have you been writing?" asked Riley, a Grade Four student.

Outside the window of the library just then, a noisy snowplow rumbled by.

"Since I was about seven years old," replied Arthur Good. He thought Riley said *riding* not *writing*. It just so happened that Arthur Good had a stable of horses and was a champion rider. Maybe that was why they were so interested in me, he thought. Maybe that's what this is all about. He could answer these questions. No problemo.

"Next?"

"What advice would you give to someone who wanted to be a writer?" asked Prissy Douglas. She wanted to be an actress and a dancer and maybe an archeologist but she asked the question anyhow. Again, Arthur Good heard the word as *riding* instead of *writing*.

"Practice, practice, practice," he replied.

All the teachers nodded in approval.

"And timing," he continued. "A sense of rhythm is important to a rider."

Of course the students and staff all heard the word writer instead of rider.

"Did anyone encourage you to be a writer?" It was Danielle, one of the bumbling bumble-bees from Primary.

"What a great question," said Arthur Good. "Yes, my father. He taught me everything I know. I lost him last year," he added sadly.

"Are you going to find him?" asked Danielle.

Arthur Good laughed. "I mean he di–" He stopped and looked at Mrs. Reed for help. He did not want to start talking about death and dying.

"Danielle, I'll talk to you later about this, okay?" said Mrs. Reed. Danielle nodded.

"Have you won awards with your writing?" asked Tobias.

"Yes. I have many ribbons and trophies."

"What do you like best about writing?" asked Simon.

"The feeling of freedom," replied Arthur Good. "When I am riding, I forget about all my worries. I love the wind on my face as I gallop along and the whole world seems to open up to me."

"He is so poetic," sighed Mrs. Reed.

"Do you ever find it difficult?" asked Aaron. He found reading and writing difficult. He was very smart in lots of ways, but reading was not easy for him.

"Oh, yes, but that is my favourite part," said Arthur Good. "There are many obstacles that I face each time I ride. But with practice I get over the hurdles and jumps, the ditches and streams. You just stick to it until you have perfected your own way of doing things."

This made Aaron feel good. He was practicing his reading and writing hard. Sometimes he felt like he was in a ditch trying to climb out. He was using the strategies he learned in Resource. Mrs. Day, the resource teacher, smiled at him and gave him a thumbs up.

Prissy seemed impressed too.

So Aaron decided to ask another question.

"How much money do you make writing?" he smiled. The teachers gasped with embarassment.

"Aaron, that is a rather impolite question," began Mr. Tiggle.

"Not at all. I don't mind," said Mr. Good. "Actually, it is a very practical question. People need money to live. Some years are better than others. It all depends. I do have a lot of overhead. Sometimes, I actually put out more money than I make from riding. There is a lot of equipment needed to keep things in order. Money buys my oats as well."

Everyone laughed at this. Arthur Good did not know why, but he joined them.

"Do you know Canary Wilson?" asked Angela finally. "She is my favourite author." She saw Mrs. Reed's eyebrows shoot upwards.

"She's my favourite author, too!" said Mr. Good warmly. "And she just happens to be my next door neighbour. She is also my good friend. She spent a lot of time at my house when she wrote her last book, *The Horse that Mooed*.

"Wow!" said Angela. "Do you think she would visit us sometime? Could you ask her?"

"I will certainly tell her what an exceptional school you have here!" nodded Mr. Good. "I know she is very busy, but I will pass

on your request." Angela and Mrs. Reed both said "Yes!" at the same time.

"Do you have any hobbies?" asked Mr. Potion.

"Kayaking, scuba diving, parachuting and mountain climbing," replied Arthur Good.

"Wow!" said everyone at once.

Then everyone wanted to know stories about his kayaking and scuba diving and parachuting and mountain climbing.

Arthur Good could tell good stories and talk for ever about his adventures.

Everyone in his audience gave him their full attention. Except for Mr. Tiggle. "Must be nice," he muttered to himself. "Freedom, adventure. What a life a writer leads!"

Everyone seemed to forget that the library smelled funny. Except for Mr. Tiggle. "Miss Argyle was right. He is a little bit too much. He's really overdone it with all that grease on his costume." He hissed this under his breath.

No one seemed to notice the room was getting colder. Except for Mr. Tiggle.

Without anyone noticing him, he left the library and went to look for Mr. Bob to ask him to turn the heat up.

Little did he know how heated up things were about to get.

Chapter 15
Impossible! Imposter!

Arthur T. Inkpen stopped writing and cracked his knuckles.

He looked at his paper.

He crossed out. He wrote a bit more.

He erased. He wrote a bit more.

He stopped.

He read out loud.

He yawned.

He threw down his pencil.

He stood up.

He did three jumping jacks.

He sat down.

He wiggled his neck from side to side.

He picked up his pencil.

He threw it down.

"I guess that's as far as I'll get for now," he sighed. It always made him a bit sad when his brain stopped working. It was like a stop sign appeared suddenly in his head. It was as if his brain hollered down, "No more juicy thoughts coming down the tubes at the moment. That's all for now, Mr. Inkpen!"

Arthur T. Inkpen also knew, however, he'd gotten a good bit of writing accomplished. He felt satisfied and full, as if he had just eaten a delicious meal.

Suddenly, however, his teeth began to chatter.

He noticed it was cold.

He poked wood into the woodstove hoping school would soon begin.

When Mr. Tiggle entered the furnace room, he was startled to see Mr. Bob dressed so brightly. For a moment he thought he'd opened a comic book and stepped inside.

"Mr. Bob, is the furnace not working?"

"Mr. Bob's up at the high school," said Mr. Inkpen turning around.

Mr. Tiggle's shook his head from side to side, like he was trying to get water out of his ears. He blinked fourteen times in a row. But the stranger was still there when he stopped shaking and blinking.

"Whatsyoukumeinwhcha!" he sputtered.

"Do you have a problem?" asked Arthur T. Inkpen, very concerned about the man with the strange movements and the strange green face and the strange language.

"I certainly do!" said Mr. Tiggle in his strictest principal voice. "My problem is you! All visitors are supposed to report to the principal's office and state the purpose of their visit. I am the principal and I know for certain you did not report to my office upon your arrival. Miss Argyle would have summoned me. We just don't let strangers walk into our school off the street. We have policy. Who are you and what is your business here?"

Arthur T. Inkpen felt as if he was shrinking. He was getting smaller and smaller and smaller. He was ten years old all over again. He was in the principal's office, because he had been day-dreaming again and did not do his math homework.

"Well, I am Arthur T. Inkpen," said Arthur T. Inkpen. "I was invited to the school for an author visit. I write books. For children." He gulped. He had a lump in his throat, like he'd swallowed a baseball.

"Imposter!" yelled Mr. Tiggle. "Arthur T. Inkpen is here. Upstairs. Telling stories in our library at this very moment."

"Impossible!" squeaked Arthur T. Inkpen. He was confused. Then again, he was often confused. He was always confused when he had been writing for any length of time.

He took a deep breath.

His wife had taught him to do this whenever he was upset or confused. He blew it out like he was pretending to be the North Wind.

"Let's start over, shall we? There's really no need to raise your voice."

"I apologize," said Mr. Tiggle. "That is not like me. Consideration for each other is what makes a school a school. But who are you?"

"I am Arthur T. Inkpen, the author," repeated Arthur T. Inkpen. "I arrived early this morning before school started. Mr. Bob showed me in here. He made me coffee. I started writing. I am very sorry. I must have lost track of time. I did not even hear the school bell ring but . . . I think I am halfway through the first draft of my next book!" he beamed.

Mr. Tiggle noticed the label on Arthur T. Inkpen's overalls. He read "Mr. Fix-it!"

"Oh no!" he began as things began to unravel in his head. "It's pot nossible!" he shouted.

"No, I am not Pot Nossible. In fact, I do not even know who Pot Nossible is," said Arthur T. Inkpen. "In fact, I have never even heard of such a weird name in all my life! And . . . you are raising your voice again!" he yelled. His face was turning as orange as the orange in his overalls.

Just then Mr. Bob came whistling into the furnace room.

"What have we here? A boxing match?"

The two men turned to him with relief.

"Tell him who I am," said Arthur T. Inkpen.

"You? Well, I didn't catch your name. But . . . well, you are the furnace repair man. Haven't you fixed it yet?" he said disapprovingly.

"You expected me to fix the furnace . . . a . . . a . . . furnace repair man?"

"Like, hello!" said Mr. Bob. "If a furnace man can't fix the furnace then who can?'

Arthur T. Inkpen began to laugh. "Oh, I get it! You are playing a joke on me right? Like if Mr. Fix-it can't fix it, who can? Right? It's a joke!"

"This is no joke," said Mr. Bob frowning.

"You can say that again," mumbled Mr. Tiggle.

"This is no joke," said Mr. Bob again.

Mr. Tiggle felt the bugaboos laughing all around him.

Arthur T. Inkpen wanted to be back home with his wife and child. Safe and sound.

Chapter 16
ATTACK!

By the time Arthur T. Inkpen and Mr. Tiggle knocked on the library door, they were chatting like old friends. Arthur T. Inkpen had complimented Mr. Tiggle on his poems and had the collection tucked away in his briefcase.

Mrs. Reed went to the door.

"Shhh! Talk in a whisper. The author is telling us about the time he met a bear when he went mountain climbing. What an exciting life he has led."

"Mrs. Reed," began Mr. Tiggle. "You won't believe what has happened."

As he began to explain, Mrs. Reed's smile turned to a frown, then to the look of someone who has just been watching a horror show, and finally, her lower lip began to tremble.

"It's . . . it's . . . it's . . . a nightmare!" she murmured and ran to the washroom. She splashed cold water on her face.

She pinched herself.

She was wide awake.

"After all those plans! After all my work! The day is a complete disaster."

She blew her nose.

It was more like a honk than a blow.

She touched up her make-up.

She walked bravely back towards the library.

She could smell the lunch that was being prepared by the homeroom parents.

She could smell pumpkin pie. So many people had worked so hard.

She was so embarrassed.

She began to sniffle again as she walked towards the library.

Her husband, Arnie, was standing outside in the hall.

"There you are! I got away early, honey. Wow! What a great storyteller he is!"

Mrs. Reed peeked in to see everyone, including Arthur T. Inkpen, listening to every word Arthur Good was saying.

"Seems like your morning was a huge success!"

Mr. Reed was quite startled when his wife began to laugh.

"What is that sound?" asked Arthur Good suddenly interrupting his story.

"It sounds as if someone is laughing."

All eyes turned to the back of the room.

They strained their necks to see the commotion in the hallway.

Mr. Tiggle sprang to attention.

He went over and whispered in Mr. Good's ear.

Mr. Good began to laugh. When he did he snorted like a horse.

Mr. Tiggle laughed and so did Arthur T. Inkpen.

"What so funny?" muttered Aaron.

"Listen to the way he laughs," giggled Prissy. Then she began to giggle like someone had pressed a laugh button on her stomach.

Then the bumbling bumblebees all twittered. The Grade Fours broke up. Mr. Potion started to choke and cough and grunt.

Mr. Long laughed like an accordian. In and out. In and out.

Soon the whole room was filled with laughing, sputtering staff and students and hardly anyone knew why they were laughing. The more they laughed the more they laughed harder. It was like the whole school had been attacked. Not by the bugaboos. By a tickle monster.

Chapter 17
Mr. Fix-it Fixes the Mix-up

Mrs. Reed, still laughing, peeked inside the library.

"Everyone is so happy, honey," said her husband. "And it's all because of you!" he beamed proudly.

Mrs. Reed laughed harder. She laughed the same way she blew her nose. Loudly. She always said it was because librarians had to be quiet so much of the time. When librarians decided to be noisy, they really let it all out.

The parents came out of the lunch room to see what was going on.

Miss Argyle came running from the office. She had been sniffing the bugaboos all morning.

Mr. Bob came running up from down-stairs. He was almost out of wood for the wood-stove. Where was that furnace man, anyhow?

Mr. Tiggle finally began to speak.

"Everyone, everyone!" he began. "Please — we have another story to tell you! It's a real comedy!"

Arthur T. Inkpen and the furnace man were shaking hands.

The furnace man gave the author his handkerchief to wipe the tears of laughter from his eyes and the author smudged himself with grease. He looked like a raccoon. This made Mrs. Graves, who was the only one who had not been laughing, start to crack a smile. Soon she was the only one in the room laughing.

"Just like the hyena in my story," thought Arthur T. Inkpen.

"Mrs. Graves, please," said Mr. Tiggle, trying to restore some order.

Mrs. Graves covered her mouth and swallowed her urge to keep laughing.

"Words, words, words," began Mr. Tiggle, "and the worlds that words can bring us. Today we have had lesson about how even one word, or even one letter in a word, and even one name can make all the difference in the world."

He began to tell the story of the mix-up of the morning.

Mr. Tiggle gave a speech that would have made a prime minister or a queen or a president famous for forever.

He talked about how when things go wrong maybe it is for a reason.

He talked about how they discovered that a furnace repair man was a man of many talents. He invited Arthur Good to revisit the school in the spring.

Arthur Good said he would bring one of his horses and charge money for rides to raise money for bringing Canary Wilson to the school.

Mr. Tiggle asked Arthur T. Inkpen if he would stay for the afternoon and read from a book that had been started right under the roof of Upper Millidocket Elementary School.

Arthur T. Inkpen said he would be delighted and furthermore, when his book was finished, it would be a book dedicated to this school.

Mr. Tiggle said that even though the day had turned upside down and inside out they were all grateful for the efforts of the best librarian a school ever had: Mrs. Reed!

Everyone cheered.

Mrs. Reed said, "God bless us one and all." Then she added, "This morning has taught me the importance of storytellers in our community. I am going to start scheduling a weekly storyteller to come and visit us as well as planning other author visits. So ask your grandparents, ask your doctor, ask your uncle who works in the mine, ask anyone who has a story to come in and let us listen!"

Then Mr. Tiggle said, "It's lunch time and everyone is invited to the staff room. Even the students!"

"Hip! Hip! Hooray!"

The parents ran back to prepare for the stampede of hungry happy staff and students.

"The furnace? The furnace! Who will fix the furnace?" protested Mr. Bob.

"Not to worry," said Arthur Good. "I'll do it right after lunch."

"But," he added, "I'm gonna need a helper. How about you, Aaron?"

He grabbed Aaron by his collar, just before Aaron was about to pull Prissy's ponytail.

"I'd love to," said Aaron. He liked looking inside of engines and motors and electrical things. "Will you tell me about scuba diving too?"

"Sure thing," said Arthur Good.

"I discovered this morning that when you have stories, you need someone to tell them to. Maybe Arthur The Inkpen will give me tips and I'll start writing some of them down."

"That's Arthur T. Inkpen, not Arthur The Inkpen," said Mr. Tiggle carefully.

He understood how easily it was to hear letters and sounds in different ways. Maybe Arthur Good makes earslips the way I make lipslips, he thought. Language can be such a tricky business.

"Anyhow," said Arthur Good to Aaron, "although it was fun to be an author for a day, I must say I'm pretty happy doing what I do."

Mr. Tiggle nodded and sighed.

Perhaps he would never get to be an author.

Not even for a day.

The bugaboos had invaded the halls of Upper Millidocket Elementary School that morning for sure.

The strange thing was it really did not seem to matter all that much.

He'd fixed the whole mix-up as well as, well . . . Mr. Fix-it. It was a matter for a principal.

"I'm pretty happy doing what I do too," he said to no one but himself.

Then Mr. Tiggle let out a deep breath the way Arthur T. Inkpen had shown him.

"I am ho sungry! *My tame is Mr. Niggle my jelly has a biggle, I am often known to jiggle at my very own gokes. I love the sound of children laughing and lerfing as they larn, yes children are my fery vavourite folks!*"

Then Mr. Tiggle jiggled and giggled and made his lipslippery way towards the staff room. His poetry echoed through the halls of Upper Millidocket Elementary School.

He would never forget to say a poem over the intercom again.

Well, almost never.

Mr. Tiggle's Delicious Word List

eccentric

idiosyncrasy

cleansing

pun

imposter

archeologist

recitation

safari

hyena